The Afterlife Michael Jackson: A Ghostly Short Story

Holy Ghost Writer

Chapter 1

A Body Taken, a Great Man Lost

It was a typical August day in 1958 when the humble town of Gary, Indiana, welcomed a very atypical boy into the world: Michael Joseph Jackson was the eighth child and the fifth boy of an average working class family. As his lungs filled with the air of the unfamiliar room around him, and his small, dark eyes first blinked open to the light, the innocent child could not have guessed what lay in store for him. His journey was to take him down a road of fame, light, and blessings, and yet at the same time his path would be marred with potholes of isolation and loneliness.

Music was destined to be an integral part of the Jackson family's life. The ten of them lived holed up in the close quarters of a two-bedroom house, but the constant togetherness resulted in beautiful harmonies that drifted out onto the lawn at all hours. The children's parents—a mother who had once aspired to be a musician and a father who also performed occasionally—had keen ears and knew their family had a special musical talent to share. What they didn't know was that one of their children would take that gift further than the others. He would stretch his God-given gift beyond the microphone, reaching all around the globe with the message of his songs.

The group that would become a sensation first started as a trio, but when Katherine and Joe decided to add two more brothers, the result was a perfect, magical quintet that soon caught on like wildfire. Though he was just five years old, shy and timid Michael was to eventually stand apart from the others, not likely because of pure talent—God knows the family was erupting with talent—but because Michael had an extra spark within him that the whole world could see. He had something more than just charisma and an astounding voice—he had a purpose behind his talent that would lead him to international fame.

He was to be the legend of the century, an inspiration to artists of all kinds, and a shining ray of light to many the world over. Yet he would face controversy and sadness as well.

Sticks and slingshots. Toys and stuffed animals. Mud and games. These are the things childhood should be made of. Oh, to be running around without a care in the world! But the young boy who looked at himself in the mirror didn't realize his childhood was supposed to be effortless and joyful. Instead, he rubbed at the bruises others left on his body and tried not to hear the harsh and cutting words said to him. Entering the world of entertainment was not a pretty business. It wasn't fair. It wasn't right—especially for a child who had no choice. But later he would reflect on these painful moments and realize they were the driving force that spurred his success and the development of his talent. The cost was high for a young boy, but it would pay a priceless reward to the world; that boy would grow up to touch hearts and lives.

Some may even consider Michael to be the modern Mozart of our time. Just as Mozart's father pushed his son ruthlessly and harshly onward to fame, so everyone around him pushed Michael. Producers, family, record labels . . . all put mounting pressure on the rising star. Rather than becoming a virtuoso of piano, like Mozart, Michael became a virtuoso with his feet—of dance. Between his high, clear voice and his startling talent for innovative choreography, he would become the King of Pop. He would develop countless fans and a cult following throughout his life. People would listen to his songs for inspiration and solace. The beat of his music would bring joy and light.

The image of the performing pop star on stage obscured the real man behind the curtain, however. The audience's applause made Michael blush. He shied away from media interviews. The shy, timid boy would grow to a man who had a vision of saving the world: "If politicians can't do it, I want to do it. We have to do it. Artists, put it in paintings. Poets, put it in poems, novels. That's what we have to do. And I think it's so important to save the world." And so the legend of a century would transform the world, pushing on to enrich a civilization where he saw people who were desperate for virtue and inspiration. A man who can handle fame and money with grace and wisdom is truly a diamond in the rough—and Michael was such a man. His guiding force of integrity and ethics would shine through his songs, his messages, and his outreach.

Fame would be Michael's platform. In 1979 he experienced the success of a worldwide, best-selling record—four more would follow, with one of them claiming the title of the biggest selling album of all time. The coveted Rock and Roll Hall of Fame would be graced by his presence twice. And award after award poured in: "Most Successful Entertainer of All Time," Songwriters Hall of Fame, eighteen World Music Awards, and thirteen Grammies. The list grew and grew. In addition to his awards, Michael found that leaders in other countries sought out his companionship. He was crowned prince of the Anyi people and the King of Sanwi, and was befriended by the prince of Bahrain.

Michael's rags-to-riches story, so unique and inspiring, seemed like it was lifted from the pages of a novel. From living in a tiny, crowded house to owning a Neverland playground built to satisfy anyone's wildest childhood fantasies, Michael had amassed fortune enough to buy anything he wanted. But his moral compass guided him not only to live for himself and his dreams, but to give happiness to others. His influence on younger generations through his music and humanitarian efforts was unparalleled. He touched countless individual lives through his Heal the World Foundation and his HIV/AIDS awareness advocacy; he also held successful benefit concerts for War Child, Kosovo refugees, UNESCO, Nelson Mandela Children's Fund, and Red Cross. He wanted children to have the joy and happiness that each young spirit deserves.

No matter how hard and unforgiving his life may have seemed at times, he never slowed down in his quest for artistry or charity. He continued to shine, despite the media's often-accusatory focus on his appearance and relationships, both of which grew increasingly controversial. Many in society couldn't accept the evolution he chose to undergo, transforming himself from a brown-skinned, round-faced boy to a white, thin-framed man. They didn't approve of his relationship choices. They couldn't understand how he connected with the people he did. But it was simple—Michael sought out the pure of heart, the innocent.

A passion for his music, his dance, and the world around him burned inside, fueling Michael's creativity. A harsh childhood may have pushed him into the business, but he later found his own guiding force. The purity of this drive led to wild success. His state-of-the-art music videos would rarely be equaled. His voice in videos melded into a perfect symbiosis of the screen, creating both culture and magic—a true expression of art. And just as poetry and symphonies continue to resonate through the generations, his art will continue to last for ages, even though his mortal body has passed. By the grace of technology, his fans still have the privilege to watch the master of pop's videos and listen to the divine flow of his rhythm.

Yet watching him now brings with it a poignant sadness—his death, like his life, was not easy or peaceful. The news shocked the world. People stopped in airports and bars to watch the news anchors share the details of Michael's passing. Those doing chores in their houses paused in front of the television to make sure they were hearing the news correctly. At fifty years old, the King of Pop, still dancing in the limelight, had now faded away?

Unfortunately, death is merciless in whom it chooses to take from the earth. There doesn't seem to be a fair equation in the universe for who goes early and who lives a long, full life. Even the brightest stars are sucked into eternal darkness in just the blink of an eye.

We can ask ourselves over and over again—why? Why did this child have to go? Why was this mother taken away? It seemed Michael still had years left of charity fundraisers to run and children to support. But life is cruel and often too short. Though the fire in his heart burned just as strongly as it ever had, it was Michael's time to go.

Still, something didn't seem right. Michael wasn't without enemies or those who sought to profit from his success—such things came as the price of fame and success. Even if that success is earned through hard work and dedication, and shared with others for a good cause, there will always be jealousy, bitterness, and anger that will hover like a dark cloud. Some accepted his death. Some questioned—looking for any coded signs he might have left, certain that his early death was caused by malice.

Of course the world would miss Michael, though it hadn't always been nice to him. Mourning rituals and candlelight ceremonies took place around the globe. It was unfathomable to most that he had been taken so unexpectedly. Tears fell for the artist, for the hero. Though he had tried to heal the pain of others, he had also experienced firsthand his own pain, caused by media, courts, and ugly attempts to tarnish his reputation.

Chapter 2

Let the Miracles Begin

Though Michael's soul had risen from his body, the heavens were not yet ready to receive him. There was still more for him to do on earth. As his spirit floated upward, leaving the cruel world behind to mourn his loss, Michael approached the pearly gates. They were as beautiful as Michael had imagined, glowing with the promise of eternal rest and peace. St. Peter stood before the gates, an imposing figure in a white robe whose thick, feathered wings unfurled behind him.

"I did not expect you so soon, Michael," St. Peter said in surprise. "But God often does not share his plans with me. Come with me, and I will lead you to Him."

Michael followed St. Peter to a shining palace made of the most perfect marble and adorned with priceless gems; inside, God waited for them. "Michael, you're here so soon," said God. "I hadn't intended for you to come this early, but your existence on earth was becoming so tortured. I have found another way for you to fulfill your destiny, and so I have called you to Me."

"Forgive me, Lord, but it was not my plan to die so young, either. I had so much good left to do, especially for the children," Michael answered. "Yet my enemies were happy to see me dead—they wanted me out of the world."

"They did," God agreed. "But they could not have succeeded in harming you if it had not been My plan to call you to My side. Don't fear, Michael. My will shall always be done. You've done a great job, and acted as my good and faithful servant. You've helped and provided for many."

"Wherever good exists, so evil will try to thwart its ways. But I'm not ready yet, God. And I left my own children without a father."

"They will be looked after. Do not worry. I knew you would not feel ready for this heavenly life, Michael, and I have another course to offer you—something that allows you to carry on with your missioning of bettering the world."

"Please, God, share it with me."

"Sometimes I send souls back to earth—not in the form of flesh and bone, but in spirit."

"I get to be a ghost?" Michael asked in disbelief.

"So to speak. Angel, ghost . . . whatever you would like to call it, you will be given specific powers to help the less fortunate. You'll be an unseen emissary for Me. But you must never engage in violence or vengeance, Michael. And once you've finished your task you'll return here to grace the heavens with your voice."

"Thank you so much for this second chance, God." In his joy Michael couldn't help but sing, and he raised his voice in a hymn from his childhood.

As he sang the last few words, he looked around, waiting for whatever was about to happen next. And in the blink of an eye, he was back on the pavement of Los Angeles, standing on the corner of La Cienega and Santa Monica Boulevard, watching the traffic go by. He swung his arm at the light pole in front of him, watching it go right through the metal fixture. He then pulled on a curled lock of his hair. Yep, that was still there. The little green man appeared on the crosswalk box, the signal for people to start crossing.

"Excuse me, ma'am?" No one glanced his direction, so Michael raised his voice. "Hey! Lady!" Nothing—it appeared that no one on earth who was living could hear him. The light turned red and another crowd gathered to wait. Michael stood with his hands in his pockets, observing those around him. Looking down toward the ground he noticed a malicious hand sneaking into the purse next to him, the woman completely unaware of the violation about to take place. Michael reached out and smacked the hand away, just as the woman moved forward with the crowd to cross over the striped pavement. The thief looked around, obviously feeling the force of the phantom hand, but unable to see where it had come from. Dumbfounded by the inexplicable feeling, the man stood still while the others moved on. Eventually he backed away and headed in the opposite direction. Michael let out a soft laugh—he had already done a good deed, in his first few minutes back on earth.

Michael raised his eyes to the heavens. "I'm not sure exactly what You had in mind as my mission, God, but I promise to pursue it and make You proud." Michael felt instinctively if he kept his focus on helping others, pursuing the goal of healing one person at a time, it would be the right path. The world should be a better place for all humans. Eradicating evil would never be possible, but still, for every small light Michael brought to someone's life, the darkness would be pushed farther away.

And yet Michael decided he would have his own side mission as well. He still had a few questions surrounding the lies, allegations, and circumstances of his own death. Seconds after Michael's heart had stopped and his soul separated from his body, Michael had known something was wrong—that it wasn't the appropriate time. Now he had the opportunity to find the gruesome details he was missing and solve the puzzle of his death. *My present situation is the perfect opportunity to find out more about the truth behind the scenes*, he thought. He was sure God wouldn't mind—after all, that was the point of free will, which was one of God's gifts to man.

Michael sat on bench and reflected on his life. His moral compass had developed into a strong and guiding force as Michael grew from boy to man. His desire to touch others' lives was never really satisfied; rather, it deepened with every good deed he did. Even as a child, he had sung from his heart and observed the suffering that surrounded him. The many problems of society touched his core, especially when the problem was related to a child who was hungry, or in pain, or otherwise disadvantaged. Something about Michael's own lack of a true childhood gave him an extraordinary compassion toward other young souls. He used his fame and money to pull people together, wake them up to reality, and push them to rally and make an impact.

Just as Michael used his songs and clear, pure voice to inspire and bring joy to his listeners, he used his money as a tool to bring awareness to the charities he championed. His honest messages about serving others for the betterment of all mankind made enemies, though. Behind the curtains of decency lie those who use their power to keep the status quo as is—so that they stay at the top in comfort and luxury. Their secret organizations have worked for centuries to maintain society in a way that most benefits them, rather than everyone. And when someone becomes a thorn in their side, like Michael, they are eager to rip that thorn out.

The names of the societies are varied—Illuminati, Free Masons, etc.—as are their jobs; some are bankers, while others are world leaders and CEOs and even actors. But their vision of the world is the same; they are driven by the madness of maintaining control. Michael's success was like a bitter drink forced to their lips. His charitable efforts brought focus to the marginalized groups whose emergence could threaten the status quo, and so the leaders of those societies had to devise a long-term plan to discredit Michael, and eventually put an end to the light that shone so brightly from him.

As a result of their clever attacks, Michael endured slander to his name and image. Accusations of child molestation broke his heart—even more so after he had children of his own. Allegations of being a traitor to his race because of the gradual lightening of his skin due to bleaching, and because of plastic surgeries that narrowed his nose, pained him. If only people really knew and understood; he wasn't trying to offend anyone with those changes. On his ascent to meet God in the heavens, he had watched as the media accused him of committing suicide to escape from debt and taxes. But there had been a force behind it all—behind every bad thing that had befallen him. It was a force he only suspected, but now he would discover it.

And so the ghost of Michael began to wander through the world, listening for and observing those in need. There was so much suffering. He wondered if one man—now one ghost—really could make a difference, especially now that he no longer had his voice or a physical form. But every person mattered, Michael argued to himself, and God would not have tasked him with this mission if He thought Michael could not accomplish it. Michael floated high into the air to look at those walking the earth, and some sorrowful voices rose to him more strongly than the others.

***

Michael stood by the bedside of a dark-skinned, dark-haired little boy who was watching TV in his bed, barely able to stay awake. The boy, Eddie, had been sick for months, with the last weeks spent in the hospital—now he was home to wait for the end of his life. Michael could read the sorrows of the little boy's heart. Eddie didn't want to leave the earth. He didn't want to leave his parents. And his Make-A-Wish, to see the one and only Michael Jackson, was no longer possible.

The boy fell asleep, dreaming of what it would have been like to meet Michael. As Eddie's eyes closed and his mind slipped off into dreamland, Michael reached out to touch the boy. Through a power God sent down from Him, a healing warmth surged through Eddie's young body. The warmth shocked Eddie's soul into the air, where it met with Michael's. Michael gave the boy's spirit a hug, and instantly the soul was completely free of disease or pain. Slowly, Eddie's soul melted back into his body, and Michael turned to leave the room.

As Eddie's eyes fluttered awake, a new energy came over him. His body no longer felt sick and weak. *Was it a trick,* he wondered. *Had the doctor come to give him a new medicine to make him feel better?* But the doctors said there was no hope—that's why they had sent him home from the hospital. Eddie thought about the dream from which he had just awoken. Michael's presence had seemed so real—as if the great performer had been right there in the room. Eddie clapped his hands; he noticed that his arms no longer shook with the effort it took to move them. Slowly, with skepticism, he swung his feet out from under the covers and settled them to the ground. He stood, moving gingerly at first and then with certainty. In another minute he was out the door and running through the backyard. He hadn't had that freedom—the freedom of childhood—in months!

His mother, washing the morning's dishes, immediately dropped the glass she was scrubbing, not even noticing when it shattered in the sink. "Howard! Howard!!" she shouted for her husband. They watched, their mouths agape.

"H-h-how is this possible? Is that our boy?" The doctor's words echoed in his head: "He has a month, at most, to live ..."

Eddie came bursting through the door. "Mom, Dad! I had a dream! Michael was in my dream and he gave me a magical hug!!" Eddie squeezed his father's waist with every ounce of strength he had in him. He did his clumsy impression of the moonwalk, singing "Beat it . . . I just beat it." The family collapsed into a mess of hugs, tears, and laughter on the floor. Eddie understood, better than the others, the miracle that had just happened.

This miracle was to be the first of many to follow, with God's touch extending through Michael's hands. He continued to walk amongst people on the street, giving invisible hugs where he saw sorrow and making small changes to people's day where he found the opportunity. Meandering down the streets of Sussex one day, he came upon a scene of terror and panic. A woman was lying on the sidewalk; she had just been hit by a tour bus. Michael reached up to touch his own cheek. *Can ghosts cry*, he wondered. *Is it possible for a tear to fall?* His spirit was saddened. As he reached the woman, her soul was standing motionless beside her, as if torn between whether to return to its earthly home or ascend to the heavens.

"Don't be sad, please. Everything is going to be okay," Michael told the woman. She said nothing, but only stared back with traumatized eyes. Her body seemed beyond repair. She began to drift further away.

"What am I going to do now?" she finally said. "My body is finished. My children—what about them?"

Michael moved in closer. He seemed to have no control over his actions. His right hand reached out to the woman's heart and again, an incredible energy came surging through his palm. He looked up toward Heaven, knowing God was working. Every living being around him, down to the birds and the bugs, could feel the change in energy.

"You will be fine. Take care of your children. They need you still."

The woman's soul melted back into the mangled body lying still on the sidewalk. The woman's heart began to beat more strongly, and her pain faded as the paramedic reached her side.

"Michael! It was Michael!" the woman mumbled as strongly as she could. The paramedics didn't pay attention to her words, but began a busy dance of rushing her into the ambulance. Everyone acknowledged the miracle of that day, though not all could understand the circumstances behind it. But the woman knew, and she told everyone who would listen—crazy though she may have seemed.

As more of these miracles happened, the word spread like wildfire. It became a topic on radio interviews and morning talk shows. The questions went unanswered: What was behind the surge of people claiming they saw Michael Jackson just before being recovering from their near-death experience? Was it a hoax? Were people making up these stories to piggyback off of the tales of others?

Michael's soul was as happy as it had ever been. He was easing the mighty suffering that plagued the earth, and he was bestowing happiness on others. *There is never a measure to say how much good there is in the world. The good deeds could be endless, and it still would not be enough. Love is strong, and only cares for joyful giving*, Michael thought. *I always believed this, but it has become even clearer now. And it's in this bliss that we cannot feel fear or dread.* Through the miracles he saw people stop their existing, and instead start living—living also to make their world a better place.

As the tales of miracles spread, the rumors about Michael's spirit on earth became an international sensation. Newscasters, conspiracy theorists, journalists, artists, and even religious leaders began to examine the many stories, looking to decipher fact from fiction. Belief in miracles revived the world over.

Chapter 3

A Sidekick

Michael loved the work God assigned to him. His soul was shining brighter than it ever had. Physical miracles would not be the only way in which he would touch lives, however. He knew his work needed to encompass more than healing the sick and the injured. Here and there he comforted the hurt, tried to reveal a clear path to the indecisive, and found ways for those in need to carry on even in the face of daunting obstacles. Each life touched could then touch another and another. *That's the beauty of love and good*, he thought. *It's inevitably contagious.*

But he saw the enormity of his task. There was just so much misery in the world. God had angels placed all over the globe, sure, but Michael had a different partner for himself in mind. A partner, helping him with his mission, would mean that twice the work could be done! It had to be someone as loved by the people as Michael was; someone who had changed the world with his or her presence, and someone who would like to return to earth give back some of the love they had received from the people.

First Michael thought of Elvis Presley. Then John Lennon. Famed singers, writers, and artists from the last few decades went through his mind. But finally . . . she was just it, the perfect choice. They had enjoyed each other so much on Earth, why not continue their journey in the afterlife together? He would ask his dearest Elizabeth Taylor. She was the woman who created the idea of stardom in Hollywood; an actress like no other. Michael had watched how people on earth were also mourning her recent death. She had been a true legend, a star who had never faded in the public eye as so many of her contemporaries. So Michael went back to Heaven to ask God for some help with his idea.

"It's up to her, Michael. If she so chooses, then I give my blessing. She just got here, you know," God said. "But go find her and tell her your plans. Anything to bring more light in the world is approved."

Michael found Elizabeth in a crowd of other souls, all of them laughing and reminiscing about life on earth. She appeared not as she had at the time of her death, but as a young and beautiful girl once again.

"Elizabeth, my love!" he called out to her. "Are you having a good time up here in God's playground, entertaining others?"

"Oh, Michael! Where have you been?" Elizabeth asked, her violet eyes shining with happiness. "I've been looking for you. I do what I know best while I'm having a good time. Oh, it's so good to see you, darling."

"Well, I've actually been hanging around Earth since I died," Michael began to explain. "I have this mission, blessed by God. . . ."

"Heal the world. I know, dear," she smiled.

"Yeah . . . " he laughed. "But the world is so big. More and more people are in need—not only of physical healing, but also of mental, emotional, and spiritual comfort. What do you think? You want to hang around as a ghost with me down there? Give back some of the love that you received? Partners in the afterlife?"

"Well," Elizabeth nodded her head slowly. "I don't know what to say. I've only been in Heaven a short time, but I do have eternity to spend here. Going back to join your mission is an intriguing offer, at least for a little while."

"Let me say these few last words to convince you," Michael said. "It's amazing to see what love can do to people. Love can change destiny. It can heal emotional wounds. It's been credited with great acts of valor throughout history. And when everything else seems lost, still faith, love, and hope remain. But the greatest of these gifts from God is love—and we can share his love on Earth, serving Him while helping others."

They talked through it some more before Elizabeth agreed to return to earth with Michael. And so the duo began their new crusade against darkness, misery, and pain. They would do their best to answer the calls of those they heard. Upon descending, their sensitive souls gravitated toward the voice of a little girl living in the snow-capped Arctic Circle. Her voice was matched with that of her mother's, making the pleas echo even louder.

Little Sarah's life had been a struggle, even before she left her mother's womb. The doctors gave her a diagnosis of a congenital malady of the brain. It would kill Sarah within the first years of her life. Yet to a mother, none of these things take away from the beauty of her baby. To her, Sarah was the most beautiful baby in the world. Despite what the doctors said, she made the decision to take Sarah home and enjoy every day that God allowed them to have together. All she could hope for was a miracle—that the doctors were wrong.

The days were hard. Watching her baby struggle and knowing that she would have to watch her little princess die before her eyes was sometimes too much for her heart to bear. But she wouldn't give up. At least Sarah was too young to understand what was happening to her. Her small body was just doing the best it could to survive—Sarah lived to be loved, not yet old enough to have any concept of the future.

The years passed and little Sarah wasn't so little anymore. Though she grew into a body that caused her pain, she had made it to the age of ten. Sarah's survival was already a miracle in her mother's eyes. The doctors were dazzled to see her grow. They rejoiced with each birthday she reached.

Due to her condition Sarah couldn't run and play the way the rest of the children did. She watched from the sidelines, cheering them on and laughing; Sarah had a brave and generous heart, and she never felt jealous that the other children could do things she couldn't. Yet almost every day she looked down at her legs and wished her body could move like the others' legs could. She wished it wasn't necessary to be so careful.

More and more the TV became Sarah's best friend. Music channels were her favorite because the joy of the beat caused her to dance inside. Though Michael Jackson was a start from little before her time, Sarah quickly picked up on his popularity. "No wonder they called him the King of Pop," she said to her mother after watching the video for "Thriller" the very first time. She was mesmerized by his singing and dancing. She could feel the rhythm right down in her soul. When she watched him she was distracted; her pain subsided and she smiled and moved her entire body to the beat. His energy on stage was like a spring of strength and inspiration. Sarah came to love Michael Jackson so much that every night she would program her iPod to one of his albums, lay the headphones next to her head, and fall asleep to his tunes.

Her favorite song became "Beat It." Singing along, she used the lyrics to voice her desire for the illness to "beat it." She would laugh sometimes as she would tell the disease to "just beat it . . . beat it." She wished so badly that she had the power to banish her disease from her body.

Sarah followed the story of Michael Jackson's supposed angel closely. She began to wish she had gotten to meet Michael, just one time. Her young spirit understood the purity of his. Though her mother disregarded the rumors of Saint Michael Jackson—as some people were calling him—as completely silly, Sarah secretly wanted them to be true. She wanted Michael to visit her and heal her.

Everything would change that December. While other children sat in their houses, watching the snow drift down, waiting for gifts, Sarah instead hoped that Michael would come and bring her the greatest gift of all: health. The large snowflakes hit her window and blurred the image of the street. It seemed the perfect time for magical things to happen.

Her iPod began playing "Man in the Mirror," and eventually Sarah surrendered to the genie of sleep.

"So what do we do with this poor little girl?" Elizabeth asked Michael as they looked inside the house.

"God will help. Just watch this."

Elizabeth took a seat on the tree branch while Michael moved through the wall.

"Hey Sarah," Michael whispered in her ear.

Her body seemed asleep, yet her mind was alert to the figure in the room. "Michael?!" she answered from inside her dream.

"I have a present for you, from God—a little Merry Christmas surprise."

Michael's soul began to shine, illuminating the room. Sarah was sure she was dreaming, but it felt so real. She tried to will her body to move toward him, but it wouldn't. Michael, instead, moved to sit on her bed.

"Don't worry. Everything is going to be just fine."

Sarah felt tears streaming down her face, still within her dream state. She went to wipe them away, yet felt no dampness on her cheeks. "How are you here? You died. Are you really here talking to me? Is this real?"

"My body died," Michael explained, "but my soul is still alive. No one really dies. We just go to another place. But God gave me the chance to stay a little longer. I still had some things on earth I wanted to take care of. God allowed me to make a change even after death, and has given me His power to heal."

"I think the Pope should make you a saint," Sarah smiled. "I heard on the news that he's thinking about it."

Michael laughed softly and shrugged his shoulders. "Everything I do is through the power of God," he said. "I myself am not divine."

"So if you're here, are you going to make me better?" Sarah asked.

"You see Sarah, I always try to help people, but only God decides who gets to be healed. And He sent me here for a reason." He gave her the kind of hug to last a lifetime.

"Now," he said as he looked around her room, finally grabbing a bowl where she kept shiny quarters. Sarah watched him stick his arm through the wall, bringing the bowl back full of fresh snow.

"Let's wait for the snow to melt. Then we'll let the magic begin."

"What magic? Is that part of how you're going to heal me?"

"Don't worry. Everything is going to be just fine. We are going to take care of everything, I promise you. You'll see soon enough."

As the snow melted, the water began shining like crystal, sending streaks of glimmering light around the room. Michael looked up toward God and began to speak, "God, you know this little girl needs a miracle. Please let these waters heal her. She deserves this." He nodded his head a few times, as if replying to a message, then handed Sarah the bowl. "Drink."

Sarah did as she was told, the whole bowl. The glowing water tasted like any other water to her. She looked up, uncertain what to expect or feel.

"Now return to your dreamless sleep, little one, and wake up happy." Michael walked through the wall, vanishing as quickly as he had appeared, joining Elizabeth outside to move on to another place.

"What a lovely little girl," Elizabeth commented, pausing to turn back and observe the small frame whose life had just changed.

Sarah woke up the next morning with a complete memory of the event. She knew it was real. She could feel deep down to her core that she was different. Her body was changed. It felt whole. She walked into the kitchen, where her mother had a special plate of food already prepared for her. Sarah devoured it quickly and hurried to the pantry for a bowl of cereal.

"Sarah dear—wha—" her mother started. She took many precautions with Sarah's diet to give her the best health possible.

"It's okay, Mommy. I'm healed. I'm fine." Sarah's mom's shoulders fell. She desperately wanted her little girl to be "fine," and she was afraid her little girl was playing an unhealthy game of pretend.

"Mom, it was Michael Jackson. He came last night. I told you he'd come. I told you the stories were true. I told you he'd make it better!" Sarah's mother silently gave her a hug, not believing. She wouldn't believe until three days later, when it was time for another MRI. Then no one else would quite believe the miracle, either. Sarah's brain abnormality was gone—absolutely gone. Her scan looked just as normal as any other ten-year-old's. Her mother could hardly believe it, sitting in the round, red leather chair of the doctor's office.

"I told you, Mom! Michael J! He did it!" And Sarah continued to tell everyone she knew as she started enjoying all the normal children's activities that she had once only dreamed of. It had been her very own Christmas miracle.

Newscasters came to visit, adding Sarah to the growing list of those who claimed to have been healed after a visit from Michael. Pressure on the Pope to make Michael a saint was mounting from those who insistently declared the legendary singer deserved sainthood.

These rumored miracles developed a cult following all their own. Festivals to celebrate Michael and his life popped up all over the world; people called on Michael to come and show himself. But Michael hadn't accepted God's mission to win glory or fame. He just wanted to continue doing what he had so desperately pursued through his music while alive—inspire and heal. So he did not appear in a physical form as his believers wished he would, but instead he quietly mixed with the crowds, touching the hearts of many though none could see or hear him. Some were disgruntled by the lack of a material presence, but others claimed they had felt his spirit touch theirs. And some recognized the presence of someone other than Michael—someone glamorously feminine.

Michael and Elizabeth eventually came to love going to these events. They would reminisce about all the times Elizabeth had visited Neverland; they had spent long nights giggling like children, watching Disney movies and acting young at heart. They enjoyed each other's presence just as much now, sharing joy as well as listening for hurt souls to touch and bodies to heal. They went anywhere they felt called. Elizabeth found it particularly thrilling to show up at AIDS benefits, just as she used to in the flesh, but this time as a ghost urging people to reach deeper into their pockets, giving researchers extra stamina and passion to keep searching for a cure.

The sun rose and the sun set and they carried on across time zones. But the thought of discovering Michael's enemies did not leave the back of his mind.

The time is now, Michael decided. *I will still carry on God's work of healing and bringing happiness—but I will take some time for my own mission each day as well. Those who have wronged me will face justice.*

He needed more information. He needed to spy and uncover their dirty tactics to control the world and squelch whatever or whoever didn't fit into their plan of power. These secret societies and the people within them were bringing darkness to the world, and Michael was determined to bring them down.

Printed in Dunstable, United Kingdom